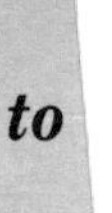

"I didn't* want *to

book," I said.

"Those pictures always make you look like a nerd anyway."

"What did you expect a bunch of nerds to look like?" asked Anthony. "Movie stars?"

That made me laugh. I was starting to feel better.

"I would mind it more if the yearbook was interesting," I said. "I mean if they had pictures that showed us the way we *really* are."

"Oh, no," said Anthony. "Can you see it?"

"We'd have a picture of Cyndy putting on makeup in the girls' room," I giggled.

"And Wally punching John every morning," said Anthony.

"You know, that's a great idea," I said. Then I started to think.

It *was* a great idea. But I was getting an even greater one . . .

Is There Life After Sixth Grade?

Leslie McGuire

Cover by Susan Tang
Illustrated by Paul Henry

Troll Associates

Library of Congress Cataloging-in-Publication Data

McGuire, Leslie.
Is there life after sixth grade? / by Leslie McGuire; illustrated by Paul Henry.
p. cm.—(Making the grade)
Summary: When her eccentric dress keeps her out of the class yearbook picture, sixth-grader Amy decides to create, with the help of her best friend Anthony's photographic skills, an alternative yearbook composed of candid shots of her classmates and teachers.
ISBN 0-8167-1706-0 (lib. bdg.) ISBN 0-8167-1707-9 (pbk.)
[1. Individuality—Fiction. 2. Schools—Fiction.] I. Henry, Paul, 1956- ill. II. Title. III. Series: Making the grade (Mahwah, N.J.)
PZ7.M4786Is 1990
[Fic]—dc20 89-20615

A TROLL BOOK, published by Troll Associates

Printed in the United States of America.

10 9 8 7 6 5 4 3

Is There Life After Sixth Grade?

To My Mother

Chapter 1

What a day!

Sixth grade was the pits. I had known it would be even before I started.

It was bad enough having to spend all day in a hot, boring classroom. It was even worse wondering if I'd make any friends this year. But I hadn't imagined an afternoon like today's in my very worst nightmares.

I couldn't believe it.

I was on the bus, minding my own business. That wasn't easy with Melissa, Cyndy and Ellen sitting right in front of me. They were laughing and yakking so loud I could barely hear myself think.

I was thinking about what a terrible day it had already been at school. It all started when I told Mr. Strickland that I thought the math reviews were stupid.

"Oh, and you know so much about math?" he said in a sarcastic voice. Mr. Strickland is my teacher. He's big and chubby, and the top of his head is bald. He grows his hair long on one side and combs it over the bald spot. But it doesn't work. I tried not to stare at his shiny head.

"Then I suppose you don't need to review," he sneered.

"It's just that school started two weeks ago and all we've done is addition, subtraction, multiplication and division," I explained. "I thought we were supposed to be preparing for junior high."

"That's exactly what we're doing, Miss Erkhardt," he snapped. "We're not all as quick with numbers as you."

I should have known he was mad at me when he called me "Miss Erkhardt" instead of Amy. But I was too fed up to notice.

"If this is getting us ready for junior high, then I'm the captain of the football team," I announced. The class laughed out loud. But Mr. Strickland's face turned red. He made me stand in the hall until recess.

"All I wanted to do was make class more interesting," I muttered to myself as I rode the bus that afternoon. Then Melissa's giggles grew even louder and I gave up trying to think.

Cyndy Weston, Ellen Bigelow and Melissa Manning are the class airheads. Cyndy spends every minute fixing her hair. Melissa never stops giggling. All three of them dress like models for *Teen Queen* magazine.

I guessed they were laughing so loud so that everyone would know they were best friends. I didn't care. They weren't my type at all. The trouble was, none of the other girls in the class were my type, either. And I knew what Ellen Bigelow would say about that.

"That, Amy," she would say in her prissiest voice, "is because you're weird."

I stared out the window and shook my head. *No matter what they say about me,* I thought to myself, *I've still got to be me.*

Suddenly I heard Melissa say, "Amy! It's your stop."

Everyone on the bus was grinning at me. The bus had stopped while I was daydreaming. Danny Miller was already at the door, getting out.

"Hurry up," the bus driver snapped.

The bus driver's name was Roberta. She had on sunglasses with tiny, round lenses, like something from a Saturday morning cartoon show.

"Don't take all day," she yelled. "I want to get home sometime tonight."

Boy! What a grouch. You'd never know Roberta drove five miles an hour in this bus. Talk about slow!

Well, I thought, I had already been yelled at by Mr. Strickland. Then the principal, Mrs. Simon, had yelled at me because my library books were late again. How could one more yelling person hurt me now?

Sixth grade was *definitely* the pits.

I got off the bus, and Roberta said loudly, "Speed it up next time, young lady." Then she slammed the door shut.

Everyone on the bus laughed and hooted. Howard Denby stuck his head out the window and yelled, "See you tomorrow, *young lady*!"

The bus wheezed off in a cloud of poisonous fumes.

Then, of course, I dropped my backpack. All my books fell out and landed in a puddle. I picked up my math book and hoped Mr. Strickland would never see it. It looked like it had been left in the bottom of a litter box for a month.

Danny Miller laughed when I tried to wipe the mud off with leaves. I was too depressed even to yell at him. I just put the books in my pack and went home.

I live in a neighborhood called Greatdale. I think they called it that because everyone there is supposed to be really great. They're not, though. What they are is really normal.

My parents are the most normal grown-ups on the block. They think normal, boring thoughts. Our house is a big, normal house full of normal, boring furniture. We even have two normal cars. Last summer I went crazy, wishing one thing around me was exciting, or at least strange.

I guess that's how I got started on clothes. My mother always bought me boring, normal clothes, just like Cyndy's, Melissa's and Ellen's. She would buy anything as long as it was fuzzy and pink.

But last summer I found a shop downtown called Secondhand Rosalie's. It was full of old dresses, blouses and skirts—really neat stuff from the fifties. I even found some combat boots there, but they were way too big for me. The best part was, all the clothes were really cheap. I could buy entire outfits with my baby-sitting money.

When I wore clothes from Rosalie's I didn't feel normal anymore. I felt exciting and strange. I would walk around Greatdale all alone and pretend I was a Gypsy fortune-teller. The other girls made fun of me, but I didn't care. They were boring, normal kids. But not me.

I decided to become a fashion designer when I grew up. But I needed practice.

I pulled out the school clothes my mother had bought the week before and laid them all out on my bed. They were the usual boring skirts and blouses, but now it seemed that all they were waiting for was a good imagination.

"I can do something with this," I muttered, picking up a dark green blouse. It had a dumb Peter Pan collar, but I liked the material.

I cut off the collar with my pinking shears so that the shirt hung off one shoulder. Then I decided it would look even better if I cut the sleeves off at the elbows and fringed the bottom. I tried it on over jeans and a turtleneck shirt.

"The layered look." I admired it in the mirror. Making new outfits was fun. As long as Mom didn't find out, I could practice fixing up my school clothes all year long.

Mom slept late in the mornings, so every

day I slipped out of the house to catch the bus without her seeing what I had on. In the afternoons she was usually off playing tennis. But today she was waiting for me in the living room. I should have expected that on a day like this one.

"Hi, Mom," I said.

Mom looked up from the magazine she was reading and stared at me. "Goodness gracious, Amy!" she shrieked. "What on *earth* are you wearing?"

"It's a skirt, Mom. My favorite!" I'd found the skirt at Rosalie's. It was made of purple felt, and cut in a complete circle. There was a poodle with fuzzy ears on the front.

Mom's eyes traveled up to my blouse. She turned pale. "What is that?"

It was my green blouse with the purple polka dots. The polka dots matched the purple skirt perfectly. But Mom didn't even notice.

"Oh, Amy!" Mom groaned. "I spend so much money on pretty clothes for you, and you go out of the house looking like a bag lady!"

That made me really mad. "It's better than looking like every other girl in the sixth grade," I said.

My mother stared at me like I'd gone crazy. Then she took a deep breath. "Your father and

I have tried very hard not to interfere with you, Amy," she said. "We know you like to express yourself by wearing old rags. But you want to be popular, don't you? Like Melissa Manning or Ellen Bigelow?"

"No way, Mom! You just want me to look like them because their mothers are your friends. I refuse to look like another cookie-cutter kid from Greatdale!"

My mother sighed. "By the way," she said. "I found this in the laundry hamper."

She held up my famous green blouse.

I gulped. "It was my very first project," I admitted.

"And the sweatpants I paid forty dollars for," said Mom. "The ones you ripped up and made into a skirt? And how about that darling green skirt I bought you? You cut the hem off, and all crooked, too!"

"That's so it will run at a slant, from my left knee to my right calf!" I explained. "Then I added a big purple ruffle. I'm going to paint some designs on it tomorrow. It'll look so amazing."

"Amy!" Mom seemed to be trying hard to control her temper. "I spent over a hundred dollars on school clothes for you this fall—"

"I know, Mom," I said. "And I really love

making them look different. Sometimes I lie in bed and just imagine all kinds of neat clothes. I've even been designing jewelry lately—"

"That's enough! I'm going to speak to your father about this." Mom sounded tired. "It's time you learned to take responsibility for your mistakes. I'm afraid we're going to have to ground you."

"Ground me? For how long?"

Mom shrugged. "A week, probably. Maybe even a month."

I gasped. "For decorating my clothes?" The more I thought about it, the madder I got. "Fine!" I said to Mom. "You can keep your old clothes! Don't bother buying me any more sweat suits! Because I won't wear them!"

"I won't have you talk to me that way," my mother said, but I was already stomping up the stairs.

I ran into my room and threw my books on the floor. Downstairs, I heard Mom slam the kitchen door.

I waited for a minute. Then I hurried downstairs.

I was so mad, I had to go out. If everybody in the world hated me, then I'd rather be alone!

Chapter 2

I made it out the door without getting stopped. That's pretty rare when my mother is mad at me. I decided to head straight down Elm Street toward the river.

Sometimes, when I'm sad, it makes me feel better to sit and watch the water go by. The river gets wide and very shallow near our house. You can see frogs sitting on their lily pads, and ducks paddling among the reeds at the river's edge. You can even see small fish swimming right near the surface. If you put your feet in the water, the fish will nibble on your toes.

Sometimes I take my sketchbook to the river

with me. I like to draw the leaves and vines. Later, I turn the drawings into designs for jewelry.

But most of all I go there when I'm in trouble. The ducks and frogs never yell at me. At least they haven't yet.

At the corner of Highland and Maple I ran smack into Anthony Williams.

Anthony is okay for someone who lives in Greatdale. That's because he wants to be a photographer. He's interested in something else besides looking and acting like everybody else, or how much stuff your parents have.

Actually, Anthony is my best friend. He's tall and skinny, and he wears glasses. They always slide down his nose.

"Hey! Slow down!" Anthony said. I'd almost knocked him off the sidewalk. "Where's the fire?"

"Under my mother," I snapped. I didn't feel like slowing down.

"Uh-oh," said Anthony. He pushed his glasses back up his nose and peered at me. "What did you do now?"

That made me mad, especially coming from Anthony. Why did everyone always think that when things went wrong, it was *my* fault? I stopped right there and turned around.

"Look, Anthony," I yelled. "No one asked you to follow me, did they?"

"But you bumped into—" he started to say. Then he stopped. He knew he had to stick up for me because he's my friend.

"I was looking for you," he said.

"Well, you found me." I started walking again. "So now you can go home."

"Boy, are you in a bad mood, Amy."

"You'd be in a bad mood, too, if all anyone ever did was yell at you for nothing."

Anthony didn't say anything. But I could see by the way his eyes got all round and innocent looking that he was thinking of some goody-two-shoes-type thing to say. I can always tell what Anthony is thinking. It's as if his head is made of glass. I can see right inside his brain all the time.

"If I were you, Anthony, I'd never commit any crimes," I said. "Your face would give you away completely."

"It would not!" he said, looking upset. "What was I thinking just now, if you're so smart?"

I smiled. "You were thinking, 'Nobody *ever* yells at Amy Erkhardt for nothing. And Amy Erkhardt is the only one who doesn't know that.' You were thinking I must have made someone really mad . . . and I guess I did."

"Okay. Look, I'm sorry," Anthony said. "What happened?"

Anthony is the only one who understands me.

"You see, I do things that *shouldn't* bother anybody," I said. "It's just that they always bother *somebody*."

Anthony squinted. "Give me an example," he said.

"Well, I suppose the biggest thing I did so far today is wear an outfit my mother didn't like."

"You always do that." He looked puzzled. "That's all?"

"Well, not really."

Anthony smiled. "Uh-oh. What else did you do?"

"Nothing much . . . I mean, nothing today. My mother just found out about it today, that's all."

"Amy. Tell me."

I tossed my head. "I cut up some clothes," I mumbled.

I was walking pretty fast, and Anthony was having to half skip to keep up with me.

Anthony always sort of flaps when he walks. His elbows flap and his shirt flaps. The way he walks makes his feet look like they're flapping, too. That's because his feet and his hands are too big for the rest of him. My father says that means he's going to grow up to be very tall.

If he gets as tall as he should get to make his hands and feet fit the rest of him, he's going to be banging his head on doorjambs.

Today he looked funnier than usual because he had his camera hanging around his neck. It bounced against his jacket. One more flapping thing looked weird.

"I didn't really cut them up," I said. "I redesigned them. But I had to cut them up a bit to do that, obviously. My mother doesn't think they look too good."

"So what else is new?" Anthony said. He'd finally caught up with me by this time. "She never thinks your clothes look good. Why are you so mad?"

"She said she was thinking of grounding me. She's also going to tell Dad that I destroyed a hundred dollars' worth of clothes."

Anthony whistled. "That's a lot of money."

"I never asked her to buy those things," I said. "I can get perfectly nice stuff for fifty cents."

Anthony glanced down at my skirt and blouse. He didn't say anything. I wasn't sure whether he liked my outfit or not.

"Look, don't worry about it," he said. "Nobody likes the way I look, either. They think I'm a nerd because of the glasses, I guess. And my parents don't really like the pictures I take. They think they're weird. My father thinks instead I should be working on that giant computer he bought me for my birthday. He wants me to grow up and be a genius computer programmer. . . ."

"Ugh," I said.

"I know," Anthony said, nodding his head gloomily. "I think I'd rather work in a junkyard or something. You can get some great shots in junkyards."

"I wonder why they don't understand that we're only happy doing what *we* like to do," I said.

"They don't understand the things we like to do," said Anthony. "If we liked to do what they liked to do . . ."

I knew just what he meant. "Or wore what they liked to wear . . . ," I said.

"Right! Then they'd have no trouble understanding us at all."

"I guess you're right."

By this time we'd reached the river. I plunked myself down and stuck my feet in the water.

"I wish I lived in New York City," said Anthony.

We'd had this conversation so many times before I didn't bother to count. But it was still a good conversation.

"Me, too," I said.

"I'd be a famous photographer, and you'd be a famous dress designer," said Anthony.

"Everyone would understand everything we do," I said.

"Instead of hating it."

"Maybe we should live in Paris," I said.

"We could live in Paris half the time, and in New York the other half."

"And take airplanes all over the world."

"And never have to talk to anyone from Greatdale again," said Anthony. "Including Mr. Strickland."

Anthony was in my class, too. There were two sixth-grade classes. Mrs. Walters taught one of them. Those kids had it easy. Mr. Strickland taught the other one. We didn't have a chance.

"That's another thing," I said. "Even Mr. Strickland hates me. That means I get yelled at all day, and then I go home and get yelled at all night. It's enough to make a person want to go to bed early."

"Weeeellll . . . ," said Anthony, "may shouldn't talk back to him like you do."

"What did I say?!" I yelled. "All I sai 'Math reviews are boring.' It's true!"

"Oh, Amy," said Anthony. "You said that if he was preparing you for junior high, then you were captain of the football team. You were showing off."

"What do you mean, 'showing off'?"

"You said that to make the other kids laugh."

"What's wrong with that?" I said. "Is laughing against the law in sixth grade?"

"No. But it's against the rules for kids to laugh at their teacher," said Anthony. "Even you could have figured that out by now."

"I make fun of Mrs. Hearth, and *she* doesn't go crazy."

"But Mrs. Hearth is the art teacher, and besides, she's different."

"You're right about that. She doesn't hate me. She likes me just the way I am."

"That's because you're such a good artist," said Anthony.

I didn't see that being an artist had anything to do with it. Mrs. Hearth is about the only person in Southside Elementary School who likes me. In fact, she's probably the one person in all of Greatdale, besides Anthony, who likes me.

Anthony sat and stared at the water for a while. Then he squeaked. Anthony always gives this funny squeak before he says something he thinks you don't want to hear.

"I don't know," he said. "I just think your life might be easier if you stopped being so mean to Mr. Strickland."

"Mean?!! Me?" I snapped. I stood up and started down the path. I was getting tired of sitting there, listening to someone tell me what was wrong with me. "I'm not mean to Mr. Strickland. *He's* mean to *me*."

"Why not try being nice to him in class and see what happens?" Anthony yelled after me. When he saw I wasn't coming back, he stood up, too. He had to start walking fast to catch up with me again.

"Don't be stupid," I said.

We walked along for a while without talking. It was getting late. I had to go home and get yelled at some more. "I guess it's good to get yelled at by lots of different people during the day," I said to Anthony. "That way you don't get as bored as you would if you always got yelled at by the same person. My mother's going to tell my father about my clothes the minute he gets home. Then he'll have a turn to yell at me."

When we were on Maple Street, Anthony stopped.

"Well, see you tomorrow," he said.

"Okay," I said. "That is, unless I'm grounded."

Anthony laughed. "Don't worry. Even when you're grounded they always let you out of the house to go to school!"

I started off down the block when Anthony yelled after me, "Don't forget to wear a white shirt and dark skirt tomorrow! It's class picture day!"

Omigosh! I'd forgotten. Now I clearly remembered Mr. Strickland standing by the door of the classroom at three o'clock. He was giving last-minute Yearbook Picture Day instructions in his jail warden voice. He was looking right at me when he gave them.

"Remember, class . . . you must *all,* and I mean *all,* wear white shirts and dark skirts or pants!"

"Anthony," I shouted. "I would rather milk a cow on Main Street than wear a white shirt and a dark skirt to school—or anyplace else, for that matter! Only nerds wear stuff like that!"

Anthony just looked at me. Then he smacked

his hand on his forehead hard enough to put a dent in it. He didn't say anything. He just turned around, muttering to himself, and went home.

Chapter 3

I'd thought the next day would be better than the one before. But I was wrong. It was so bad it could go down in history.

It was all Mr. Strickland's fault.

For one thing, I didn't even own a white blouse. So even if I'd wanted to—which I didn't—I couldn't have worn the stupid, dumb outfit he wanted for the yearbook picture. Besides, why should I look like everyone else? I wanted to be able to tell which one was me in the picture.

I admit that I did own one white sweater, but that was no help, anyway. For one thing it was really hot that day. I would have gotten all hot and sweaty in a sweater. That's why they call it a sweater, right?

For another thing, it was a fuzzy angora thing that my mom got me. It had puffy sleeves. It was itchy even though it wasn't supposed to be, and it looked totally disgusting on me.

So I did the next best thing. They wanted us to dress up and look nice, right? So I dressed up.

I had this really neat dress that I found at Secondhand Rosalie's. It was totally fifties, with a big, round skirt and a tight top with a square neckline. The only thing wrong with it was that it was *all* black. It was also too big, but taking it in was easy. I still needed some white on the top half. So I found an old fake pearl necklace in my toy chest and put that on.

I smiled at my reflection in the mirror. How neat and dressed up could I get? A pearl necklace wasn't exactly like wearing a string of African monkey teeth, was it?

But no. It was not only not good enough, it made Mr. Strickland go completely crazy.

When I walked into class, he was going over some papers. I thought he wouldn't notice me. But just as I sat down, he looked up.

"Miss Erkhardt," he said in a voice right out of a horror movie. "What do you call that outfit?"

I looked over my shoulder and saw that everyone in the class had frozen. It was like a photograph. Wally had one arm raised in the air—he was about to give John his good-morning punch. Ellen was bent over, putting her notebook under her chair. Chrissy and Sandra had just walked into the room. They stopped talking but forgot to shut their mouths.

Who could resist a question like that? Not me. What did I call my outfit?

"I call it Martha," I said, smiling sweetly.

You would have thought that I'd thrown a spitball at him. Mr. Strickland stood up really slowly, and he pointed at the door.

"Miss Erkhardt, go to the principal's office . . . this *instant*!" he howled.

Anthony looked at me and shook his head. I put my books inside my desk, and walked out the door.

I marched down the hall to Mrs. Simon's office. It was a very long march.

When I got there the school secretary, Mrs. Wild, looked up at me.

"Not again, Amy," she said. She knew I was there to get hauled in front of the principal. How did she know that? Why didn't she think that maybe I'd lost my lunch card, or that I needed to call my mother or something? Easy. Because I spent a lot of time in Mrs. Simon's office. Mrs. Wild and I knew each other pretty well.

"Have a seat, Amy." She gave me another sad look. Then she stared at my dress, and went right back to her typing.

I sat on the bench and waited. Ten minutes later, Mr. Strickland came charging in.

Mr. Strickland liked to pretend that he really should have been a college professor instead of an elementary school teacher in a little suburb. He wore tweed jackets with leather elbow patches. Sometimes I even saw him smoking a pipe as he walked out to his car after school.

He glared at me and said, "The rest of the class has gone down to the auditorium to have their picture taken. You, young lady, will not be part of that. You didn't follow instructions, and as far as I'm concerned, you will not have a picture in *our* yearbook."

"Are you sure that's fair?" asked Mrs. Wild. She looked really unhappy for some reason.

Maybe she thought the only reason anyone went to school was to get their picture in the yearbook.

"It certainly is," said Mr. Strickland. "Miss Erkhardt can't have her own way all the time. If she won't obey the rules, then she'll have to pay the price. I am extremely upset!"

I could tell he was upset because he'd gotten his hair all messed up. The long hair that was supposed to be combed over the top was hanging over his ear instead. He looked really weird. I tried not to laugh, but it didn't work.

Mr. Strickland heard me. He stomped right up to Mrs. Simon's door and marched in.

I would have thought he'd knock first.

He slammed the door behind him. I heard some mumbling behind the door.

Mrs. Wild looked at me as though I had murdered all the kindergarteners. After all, what could I have done that was so bad that I wouldn't be allowed to have my picture in the yearbook? She should only know. Of course, she *would* know, soon enough.

After about three minutes, the door opened again.

"Miss Erkhardt," said Mr. Strickland. "Would you please come in here?"

He turned to Mrs. Wild. "Would you bring Amy Erkhardt's permanent record in here?" he demanded.

Uh-oh, I thought as I went in. My permanent record probably listed every time I ever got sent to Mrs. Simon's office. All those red marks probably made me look a lot worse than I really was.

Mrs. Simon was sitting there, looking sad and sort of tired.

"Oh, Amy," she said in that gloomy, disappointed voice she'd get when you'd done something bad. "What are we going to do with you?"

I felt sorry, but not about the dress or Mr. Strickland. I was sorry that Mrs. Simon was unhappy. Mrs. Simon wasn't bad. It was just that she always made you feel that you hurt her feelings. That felt worse than being in trouble for whatever it was that you did.

"I don't know," I mumbled, looking at my feet.

"Sit down, dear," she said. "I'm afraid I'm going to have to call your mother."

I sat there while she called home. The talk she had with my mom was too short. That meant Mom would be there in about thirty seconds. And mad as a bee, too.

While we waited, I listened to Mr. Strickland go on and on about what a terrible kid I was. How I made it impossible to teach. How I disrupted the class, and how I daydreamed all the time!

Personally, I couldn't see how it was possible to daydream all the time and disrupt the class all the time, too. I don't disrupt the class. I hardly ever said a word! John Millsap was yakking all the time in class. That's why Wally punched him every morning. He wanted John to start the day by shutting up. But it never worked.

And did John Millsap ever get in trouble? Nope. Only me, because I made a wisecrack now and then.

I think that was because John Millsap was a stupid boy, and Mr. Strickland liked stupid boys. They must remind him of what he was like when he was a kid. What Mr. Strickland didn't seem to like was smart girls.

Oh well. I sighed. Sixth grade couldn't last forever.

I didn't have to wait long for Mom, which was good. I was tired of listening to Mr. Strickland complain.

My mom came racing in the door, wearing her tennis outfit. She looked really steamed.

"Now what?" she snapped. She bounced the tip of her tennis racket on the floor. "I don't have much time. I'm due at the country club in ten minutes."

She frowned at me as if this was all my fault. How could I help it that no one liked my outfit?

Mr. Strickland started all over again from the beginning. He ended up his speech by pointing at my dress, and saying, "And Amy had the nerve, the *audacity*"—he liked big words—"to come to school dressed like *this* for the yearbook pictures!"

My mom looked at my dress. Mrs. Simon looked at my dress. Mr. Strickland looked at my dress. They looked at it for about a year. You'd think no one had ever seen a dress before.

"That's it, young lady," my mother snapped. "Tonight your father is going to have a talk with you about this clothes business."

"It's not the clothes exactly. It's more . . ." Mr. Strickland started to say.

I knew he wanted to talk about my "behavior." But when Mom gets going she's even tougher than Mr. Strickland.

"The clothes are the worst part of it," my mother insisted. "We try to be good parents.

We give Amy almost everything she wants. We simply don't know what to do anymore." She looked sad.

Mrs. Simon started to get fidgety. Maybe she had some real work to do instead of listening to my mom get crazy about outfits.

"I think it would be a good idea," Mrs. Simon said, "if you and Amy and Mr. Erkhardt settle this at home, Mrs. Erkhardt."

What Mrs. Simon meant was: stop talking about it in my office.

My mom stood up and got her tennis racket.

"I don't have time for this, either," she said. She looked at me. "We'll finish discussing this when you get home from school. My tennis lesson started seven minutes ago." Then she stormed back out the door.

By the time all this was over, so was the picture-taking session. I didn't get into the shot, and I went back to class feeling totally terrible. Not that I wanted to get in the yearbook. But everybody acted as if I had some awful disease. The whole class was really quiet all morning. They were busy staring at me.

At lunch, I finally got to talk to Anthony.

"I don't want to be in the stupid yearbook," I said. "Those pictures always make you look like a nerd, anyway."

"What do you expect a bunch of nerds to look like?" asked Anthony. "Movie stars?"

That made me laugh. I was starting to feel better.

"I would mind it more if the yearbook was interesting," I said. "I mean, if they had pictures that showed us the way we *really* are."

"Oh, no," said Anthony. "Can you see it?"

"We'd have a picture of Cyndy putting on makeup in the girls' room," I giggled.

"And Wally punching John every morning," said Anthony.

"You know, that's a great idea," I said. Then I started to think.

It *was* a great idea. But I was getting an even greater one. I jumped up.

Anthony looked at me as if I'd just lost my marbles. "Oh, no. Amy, whatever it is, I don't want to get involved!"

"Then don't," I said. "But at least listen to my idea before you turn it down. This might be your big break! It could turn you from a nothing kid in Greatdale to the most famous photographer in the world!"

Anthony started to look interested.

"This is what we do," I said. "We make an alternative yearbook. We—you and I, that is—go around and take pictures of all the sixth graders, the teachers, the lunchroom staff, everybody! Not just regular pictures, either. We'll catch them when they're not paying attention."

"I get it," Anthony said slowly. He started to smile. "We'll get candid shots of everyone that show all the things they *really* do!"

"You got it!" I said, nodding. "All the *dumb* things. And we'll have sneak interviews. We'll ask kids what they think of other kids. That way we won't have to have those dumb remarks under the pictures that say stuff like, 'I want to be a race-car driver when I grow up.' Our book will say things like 'Terry should learn how to chew with his mouth closed!' "

Anthony started to look weird again. He let out a little squeak.

"I don't think we should say things that are too mean," he whispered.

I looked at him. I felt like telling him to stay out of my yearbook. But then I thought about it. Anthony was my best friend, and the yearbook wouldn't be any fun without him. And he was a *really* good photographer. And besides . . . he was right.

"I don't want to be mean, either," I finally said. "We'll let the pictures do all the talking.

After all, a picture is worth a thousand words, right? Especially your pictures."

Anthony had no choice but to agree with me. He smiled again. By the time the bell rang and we went back into class, I was feeling a hundred percent better.

Chapter 4

By Thanksgiving, Anthony and I had a pretty good idea of how to handle the yearbook. We worked on it every day, and Anthony always had his camera ready.

I was on probation at home, but so far things had been quiet. Maybe too quiet. The only problem I had was that at the beginning of the week, I forgot myself and made a joke in class. Mr. Strickland didn't say anything to me about it. He just glowered at me. Of course, he was still glowering at me three days later. I figured he was mad at me again. But at least he wasn't doing anything.

As soon as the school bus let us off, Anthony and I headed straight for the river. It was cold and gray, but we needed to talk about the yearbook.

"We'd better call it something else," I said. "*The Alternative Yearbook* isn't exactly the snappiest title I ever heard."

We thought about that awhile. We had to come up with something really great.

"How about, the *Southside Other*?" asked Anthony.

"The *Southside Other,*" I repeated. "Not bad, but it sounds like a horror movie."

"Well, we have to think of some word that means this yearbook is the *other* yearbook," he said. He was crabby that I didn't go nuts for his idea. "What else means *other* besides *other*?"

"Substitute?" I suggested.

"No. Too long," said Anthony. He thought some more. "How about, *Make Way for the Real Yearbook*?"

"That's it!" I screeched. I jumped up and started pacing back and forth. A startled frog leaped away from the riverbank.

"It is?" said Anthony. He looked surprised, too. "It's too long, isn't it?"

"Yes," I said. "But I didn't mean the whole title, I meant the 'real' part."

"What do you mean, 'the real part'?" He looked confused.

"We'll call it *The Real Yearbook*!"

Anthony started to smile. I could tell that he got it.

"Right," he said. "That'll make it look like *our* yearbook is the real one, and the one put out by the school is the phony one!"

"And our yearbook shows the kids and the school the way it *really* is!" I added. "Good thinking, Anthony." I believe in giving people credit for being smart.

"It wasn't all my idea," he said with a goofy smile. "You're the one who thought of it, Amy."

"It was both of us," I decided. "We make a good team."

He beamed at me for a second. Then he started to look gloomy.

"Where are we going to get the money for all this?" he asked. "I only have eighteen dollars left over from my birthday money."

I had to admit that he had a point. After all, film cost money. Getting all the copies made cost money, too. In fact, everything would cost more money than either of us had. And we weren't going to sell *The Real Yearbook*s—we were going to give them away.

"I have twenty-eight dollars," I said. "How much is eighteen and twenty-eight?"

"I don't think it's enough," said Anthony.

I did some quick thinking. "That adds up to forty-six dollars," I said. "Maybe that's enough to get started."

"Where does the school yearbook's money come from?" asked Anthony.

"I don't know," I said. "Maybe from the Parents' Association."

Just then, Anthony's gloomy expression vanished. He looked like a light bulb had lit up over his head. "Wait a minute," he said. "There are ads in the back of yearbooks . . . remember those?"

"Oh yeah!" I frowned. But who would want to place an ad in a yearbook that wasn't the official one?

"Maybe parents," said Anthony, looking at me. "Parents who have businesses."

I thought about it for a minute. My father had a business . . . an advertising company. Actually, that meant he would know other people who might place ads in the yearbook, too!

"I'll get my dad to buy space!" I said.

Anthony made a squeaking noise. "Do you think your dad will do it?" he asked, giving me his famous doomed-out look.

It was true. My dad wasn't exactly delighted with me. Especially not after my mom got finished talking to him last month. But I hadn't cut up any clothes lately.

"Maybe you should tell him that doing this yearbook is a way of doing better at school," said Anthony hopefully.

"You mean, make it sound like this project is going to straighten me out?"

"Right," said Anthony. "It might be good if you said a teacher was helping you work on it. . . ."

"Like Mrs. Hearth!" I said.

Anthony smiled. Then he started to look gloomy again.

"But you haven't asked her," he mumbled.

"I'll just have to say I did," I snapped. I said it so loud, I startled another frog. The frog jumped off the edge of the embankment. It landed with a plop in the water and splashed a duck in the face.

"What if Mrs. Hearth *won't* help?" Anthony squeaked.

I gave him a look that would have turned anyone else into a lamppost.

"Mrs. Hearth will help me," I said, trying to sound as if I knew it for a fact. Of course I didn't know any such thing. Mrs. Hearth might not want to because it really wasn't a school project.

But I was sure she'd understand why Anthony and I wanted to do it. I was sure she'd help me . . . almost.

"I think I'd better start home," I said to Anthony. "Maybe if I clean up my room first and then talk to my dad, I'll be able to make this plan work."

I practically ran all the way home. Poor Anthony had a hard time keeping up with me, even with his long legs.

Luckily for me, Mom wasn't home yet. That gave me some time to turn myself into the perfect kid.

I went straight up to my room. It didn't look too bad. The piles of stuff on the floor were only about a foot deep, so it was no problem to clean up. I even put a load of stuff in the washing machine.

Then I rearranged my desk. I figured it would look real good if I spent the next few nights working in my room. I'd be thinking up ideas for *The Real Yearbook,* of course. But my mom would probably think I was doing homework.

Not that work or grades have ever been a problem for me. I always got good grades on all my tests, and I always did my homework. That part was the easy part. The hard part was keeping myself from making remarks to the teachers. That's what got me into the most trouble at school. That's why I always got a U (which is highly unsatisfactory) in citizenship, obedience, attitude toward self, attitude toward peers, attitude toward adults, attitude toward learning (which they think is different from just plain learning) and self-control.

I got an S+ or O in practically everything else.

Grown-ups get very confused when their kids get good marks but have a bad attitude. They think if the kids are bad at one thing they have to be bad at everything. Hah!

But this time they'd think I really cared about school again.

By five o'clock my room looked like a museum. No real kid could possibly live in it for more than five minutes.

I heard the door bang shut. Rats! My mom was home. I couldn't decide whether to go downstairs and talk to her, or to hide in my room until I heard Dad come in.

I chose going downstairs. After all, she might come looking for me, anyway, so what could I lose?

When I got into the kitchen, Mom looked at me. I was wearing the green skirt I'd redesigned. Big mistake. I should have changed. She started stamping around, slamming doors and banging cans down on the countertop. I guess she wasn't feeling very calm.

"Hi, Mom. I cleaned my room," I said.

"That's nice." Mom banged a box of frozen spinach down on the counter. Then she banged a box of frozen fish next to it, and a container of frozen sauce next to that. Mom feeds us so much frozen food, Dad calls her Nanook of the North.

"Is something wrong?" I asked.

"Yes, young lady. As a matter of fact, something is." She glared at me. Then she dropped a bombshell.

"I got a letter from Mr. Strickland today," she said. "It's about your attitude. Mr. Strickland says he thinks you're too immature for the sixth grade. He says you've been acting up to get attention. He says—" She looked like she was about to cry.

"He says that if you don't start behaving better, you might not graduate to junior high."

I stared at her. "But my grades—"

"Your grades aren't all that's important!" said my mother. "Not if you can't act normal!"

She stopped yelling and took a deep breath. "I've asked Dad to come home early tonight," she said. "He wants to talk to you."

At that moment a car door slammed, just like in the movies. Dad. Home already!

Not only was my room too clean to live in, but I wouldn't have a chance to sell ad space in my yearbook.

I could have cried, but that's not my style.

"Anybody home?" Dad yelled as he walked into the house. He appeared in the kitchen doorway. He didn't look happy to see me.

"Nice suit, Dad," I said with a cheerful smile.

My dad's business suits are ironed so crisp, it's a wonder he doesn't cut himself on the cuffs. They look pretty good, even if they *do* all look exactly alike.

But my parents didn't want to talk about clothes.

First Mom yelled at me while Dad listened. Then Dad yelled at me while Mom listened. Then they said, "What have you got to say for yourself?"

I started talking about *The Real Yearbook.*

"Dad," I said, "I've always wanted to put out a magazine of my own. Mrs. Hearth says she'll help me work on a yearbook that's even better than the one I won't be in."

Dad turned to my mother. "What is she talking about?"

Mom shrugged and looked confused, so I kept right on talking.

"You see, I have to sell ad space in the back of the yearbook."

"You mean you have a job working on the yearbook as punishment for getting thrown out of the yearbook?" he said. "What is she talking about, Milly?" I could see that explaining this was going to be harder than I thought.

"There are two yearbooks this year, Dad. I'm in charge of the other one. I was hoping you might want to advertise your company in the back—you know, buy an ad or two. And you might know a few of your clients who'd like to advertise, too. . . . We don't need much money, just . . ."

I never got past the part about not needing much money. As soon as I said the word *money,* they both went crazy.

"Young lady," my dad howled, "your mother told me that just last month you cut up a hundred dollars' worth of clothes!"

"Not only that, John," said Mom. "She won't even wear them once she's cut them up! She says those clothes were just for practice. Instead she wears rags from a secondhand store!"

"That's not true!" I said. "I'm wearing the green skirt!"

Both of them stopped and looked at me. They didn't look pleased. I should have kept my mouth shut.

"Where did we go wrong, Milly?" my dad said. "It isn't as if we were on welfare. We give her everything she wants. . . ."

They were talking about me as if I wasn't even there. I hate that. I also wondered what made them think they gave me everything I wanted? Had anyone in this house ever *asked* me what I wanted? Not lately.

I sat down on the kitchen chair and rested my chin on my hand. I let them go on for a while. It seemed to make them happy.

But then came the next bombshell.

"You're absolutely right, Milly," Dad said in his gloom-and-doom voice. "If she doesn't shape up by the end of the year, and I mean *really* shape up fast—then she goes to boarding school."

"What!" I said. Now it was time to pay attention. "Hold on a second. What do you mean, boarding school?"

"We've already discussed it, Amy," said my mom. "We feel that if you aren't happy at Southside Elementary . . ."

They were right about that, but getting sent to boarding school wasn't going to make me happier. It would be a million times worse!

I started to tell them to forget it, but Mom went right on like a tractor-trailer going down a hill.

"Sunnydale Academy is famous for offering lots of discipline," she said. "It's designed especially for children who have trouble adjusting to the usual classroom. . . ."

"You mean, it's reform school," I yelled. I stood up and started out of the kitchen. I didn't want to hear any more lies about what a neato place this reform school was.

"No, it isn't," said my mom. "It's for creative children—children who need something out of the ordinary."

I didn't stay around to hear more. I didn't want to go to any boarding school!

"Shape up, Amy," my father boomed as I ran up the stairs.

But I could see there was no point in shaping up. I took all my stuff and threw it on the floor again. The room was too neat to live in, anyway. I hate a clean room.

I decided right then and there that I was going to act just the way I'd always acted. But the only difference was I was going to do a fantastic *Real Yearbook.* It would be great! It would be funny! It would be strange but true!

And then when it was done, I'd just run away!

Reform school? Forget it!

Chapter 5

Mrs. Hearth finally said she'd help us! I was pretty sure she would, but boy, was I glad when she said she'd be the adviser on *The Real Yearbook.*

What happened was this: right before Christmas vacation I asked Mrs. Hearth if I could talk to her after school. I didn't want to ask her in art class. Not in front of everyone.

"Hi, Amy," she said when I came into the art room. "What can I do for you?"

I told her about not getting my picture in the yearbook, and how Mr. Strickland and my mother went crazy because of my black dress.

Mrs. Hearth was an artist, too. She didn't

always wear the most "in" clothes, either. I guess part of the reason was that she was going to get paint and clay and papier-mâché all over herself. But part of the reason was because she liked to dress that way. Just like me. Mrs. Hearth could understand the clothes I wore. She understood why I cut things up now and then, too. That's why we liked each other so much. She still stuck up for Mr. Strickland and my mom sometimes. But she did it in a way I didn't mind so much.

"Sometimes, Amy, you just have to do what your parents want you to do," she explained. "When you grow up, which is going to be very soon, you'll be able to dress any way you want, and live any way you want."

"I know," I said. "But it's just so unfair. I didn't do anything really bad. Lots of kids do a lot worse things. . . ."

"Never compare yourself to other people, Amy," Mrs. Hearth said. Then she patted my arm. "You're different from most kids. But you're still going to have to try and live with other people." She grinned. "Besides, other kids can be nice. You should try making friends with them sometime."

Easier said than done, I thought. But that wasn't what I'd come to talk to her about.

"I feel bad about not being in the yearbook," I said. This wasn't exactly true, but it sort of was, too. "So I thought I'd like to make an alternative yearbook. One that's funny and different."

"Explain," said Mrs. Hearth.

"Anthony and I have been taking pictures of kids and teachers and the school—everything. We want to show the school and the kids the way they *really* are. We decided to call it *The Real Yearbook.*"

Mrs. Hearth's eyes lit up. "That's a great idea, Amy! But it's a lot of work."

"I know," I said. "I'd like you to help. I don't mean by doing work, but by giving us advice. Like Mr. Strickland does with the regular yearbook."

Mrs. Hearth looked surprised. For a minute, I thought she was going to say no. Then she smiled. "I'd love to," she said.

She gave me a hug. "Now sit down and tell me exactly what you have in mind. We'll start with the overall plan. Then we'll design some basic layouts. We'll start work in January, okay?"

After vacation, we wrote down how many kids were in the two sixth-grade classes, the names of the teachers who worked with them and the names of all the different activities at the school.

We listed gym and lunch, art, music, the class play, the science trip we take in March, the people who work in the office, the library . . . you name it, it was going to be in the yearbook.

We figured out how many pictures of kids would fit on each page. Then we counted how many pages we'd need for that and the comments. Unfortunately, we ended up with more than sixty pages. So we started all over again—sixty pages was way too long.

"You're going to have to get other kids besides Anthony to help," Mrs. Hearth said when we'd finished.

I didn't feel like asking anyone else for help, but I didn't tell Mrs. Hearth that. "I'll talk to Anthony," I said. "Maybe he knows of someone."

The next day at lunch, I told Anthony what Mrs. Hearth had said.

"No problem," said Anthony. "I'll ask Kurt and Debbie to help. They live on my block, and I've known them since I was little."

Before I could worry about whether Kurt and Debbie would make fun of our yearbook idea, Anthony had called them over to our table.

"We'd love to help!" Debbie said when Anthony explained the problem to them. "It sounds like a great idea!"

"I want to work on the captions to the pictures," Kurt said. "I've already thought up two great ones!"

I was pretty amazed. I'd never paid attention to Debbie and Kurt before this. But they turned out to be really funny.

Debbie had curly brown hair and big brown eyes. She was so tiny she looked about eight years old. She never said much, either. I guess that's why I had never paid any attention to her before.

Kurt was in Mrs. Walters's class. He was tall like Anthony, but not as skinny. I always thought he was just a dumb jock because I used to see him running around in his gym clothes. He was on the track team, but it turned out that he was really smart, too. He made up some great captions without even thinking very hard.

Soon, things really started to take off. Anthony taught all of us how to use cameras—checking to make sure the light was right and focusing correctly. Debbie asked her parents for a camera for her birthday. Kurt borrowed his dad's. All I had was an Instamatic, but it worked pretty well.

We took our cameras with us everywhere. That way, if something neat happened, we'd get a picture of it for *The Real Yearbook.*

And, boy oh boy, did we get some neat pictures. We shot everything that made the sixth grade a year to remember.

We got a picture of the football coach slipping in the mud when he tried to show Darrin Hawkins how to catch a pass. We got a picture of Mrs. Waters, the cafeteria lady, right after she dropped a whole tray of spaghetti and meatballs. We took a picture of the track team the day it won the race against Westfield Elementary School. That one was going to go opposite the picture of the track team the day it got totally trashed by Marshall Elementary.

But the best picture of all was the one Debbie got of Heather Wilkins—the most beautiful girl in the sixth grade—with her hair up in curlers. It was right before the class play in February. We put on a play that was written by both classes together. It was about Benjamin Franklin. It was part of our social studies unit on the American Revolution. Heather wanted her hair to be perfect just in case there were any talent scouts in the audience. So she set it in the afternoon.

That whole thing was so funny we had two

pages on it. There had to be room for quotes from the play. Like the line where Ben Franklin discovers electricity by flying a kite with a key attached to the kite string. When lightning hit the kite, and he got a shock, he said, "Like, wow! There's electricity in them clouds!"

The class trip in March also needed two pages. It was an overnight field trip for science. The whole sixth grade would be staying in a camp in the mountains. We were supposed to watch nature or something. If it hadn't been for *The Real Yearbook,* and the chance to get some great shots of people in their pajamas, I never would have gone. The thought of spending four days and three nights with Mr. Strickland wasn't my idea of excitement. But I went. And I had a really good time!

It was freezing in the mountains. There were cabins to sleep in, which was a lot better than tents. But it was still pretty rugged. We stayed six in a cabin. The only real dip in our cabin was Cyndy Weston, but she was outnumbered by Debbie and me. Joan Kirklee, Sally West and Ellen Young turned out to be okay, too.

Each day the counselors took us on walks to teach us about rocks and plants and tracking animals in the snow.

It was neat. Even the food was strange but

good—lots of grain stuff and vegetables. The beds were terrible. But the best part—at least as far as getting great candid shots—was the fact that no makeup was allowed. We thought Cyndy was going to die. They also didn't allow blow dryers or electric curlers, and no hair spray, either.

Even some of the boys freaked out because they couldn't blow-dry their hair and use gel. I didn't even know boys *used* gel! The girls walked around all day, yanking on their hair, saying, "I can't believe I look like this!" The boys all looked like nerds. We got a lot of pictures of kids going crazy trying to keep us from taking their pictures. They all had the same reaction: holding their hands out and screaming, "Get away from me!"

Anthony even got a shot of Mr. Strickland with his face half-shaved. I would have liked it better if he was brushing his teeth. After that he always kept the bathroom door shut *and* locked.

After that trip, more and more kids wanted to work on the yearbook with us. At first, Anthony thought we didn't need more kids, but there was a lot of work—and lots of typing, too. Anthony hates typing, so . . . we got more kids to help.

I started talking to kids I'd never talked to before. At first, since I knew they were either morons or nerds, I just told them what to do.

Sometimes I guess I wasn't very nice. It was just that I didn't know the kids were actually okay. Okay, I admit it: I've never been exactly popular at school. I mean, most kids wouldn't talk to me. It took me awhile to get used to them acting normal.

One day, after I'd told a bunch of kids what to do and how to do it, Anthony said he needed to talk to me.

"You know, Amy," he said. "Maybe you should ask some of them if they have any ideas."

"What for?" I said. "I bet they don't."

"You might be right, but try it. Also, maybe you should talk a little nicer to them. . . . All they want to do is help."

I glared at him. "What's your problem?" I asked.

"You're being kind of bossy, Amy."

"I am not!" I snapped.

He started squeaking. Then he said, "The kids really like you, Amy. But they think you don't like them. I told them you do, but no one believes me."

That night, I thought about what Anthony

had said. Maybe he was right. I was talking to the kids on the yearbook just the way my mom talks to me. Too bossy.

I started to laugh. I remembered a kid I saw at the supermarket one time. The mom was walking along, yelling at the kid. The kid was walking along, yelling at her doll.

"Okay, tomorrow I'll try to be nicer," I decided.

And I did. To my surprise, it actually worked.

"See what a difference it makes when we work together?" Anthony said a few weeks later. "Everyone's coming up with great suggestions!"

It was true. We ended up having to add more pages for all the funny poems and drawings. Even I did some cartoons.

Pretty soon, our files were bulging with way too much stuff for one yearbook. If we had used everything, it would have been five hundred pages long!

But the hardest part was raising money. That was where the help from all the extra kids came in very handy. In fact it was just what we needed.

"The cheapest way to make our yearbook is to get it Xeroxed," said Kurt at one of our weekly meetings. "Printing it is just too expensive."

"The pictures won't look as good if we Xerox," said Anthony.

"We have no choice," said Kurt. Everyone looked sad.

"Then the only answer," said Anthony, "is to keep our photos as light as possible. If they're too dark, they'll print like inkspots, not photographs."

"Even if we Xerox it," I said, "we'll still need about a hundred and twenty-five dollars."

"That's a lot of money!" said Debbie.

"Plus, we'll need a special kind of big stapler that goes through thirty-two sheets of paper," said Kurt. "They cost twenty-one ninety-five. Not including tax."

"So we need at least one hundred and fifty dollars," said Anthony. "Ouch!"

"I know," Debbie said. "We could sell cookies at lunch and after school. That's how the Parents Association makes money."

Everyone liked that idea. Soon, armies of kids showed up at school every day, loaded with baked goodies to sell.

By early May, *The Real Yearbook* was no longer a private project among Anthony, Debbie, Kurt and me. *The Real Yearbook* had become a class project for the entire sixth grade.

And what was really strange was that kids actually waved to me at school and said hi! I really liked it, too!

In art class one day in May, Mrs. Hearth was watching me. She grinned and said in a quiet voice, “It’s nice having friends, isn’t it?”

Chapter 6

By May 10, we sixth graders had earned a hundred and fifty dollars. That's a lot of cookies at ten cents each. In fact, it's exactly 1,500 of them!

By that time, we were almost ready to put *The Real Yearbook* to bed, too. That was what Mrs. Hearth said it was called when you were ready to print something. She said printers called it that because the platform of the old-time presses were called beds.

The only chore left was to type the names of all the kids in the index on the last two pages. It was a yucky job. No one was very good at typing. No one wanted to do it—even if we divided it up.

I decided to be the good guy, and do it all myself.

"After all," I said to Anthony, "I'm the best speller in the class. At least you know I'll do the job right." All I needed was to make a list of each person who appeared on each page of the yearbook. Then I'd put the names in alphabetical order.

On May 10, that was the biggest problem we had. We thought it was pretty big. But we were in for a big surprise.

It was actually all my fault. But how was I supposed to know that Mr. Strickland would go into the art room at four-thirty in the afternoon? How was I supposed to know that he would see the layouts and flip through them? And how was I supposed to know that after that he'd even look through our files and find all the silly comments we'd decided not to use, too?

I guess I knew that if he read all that stuff he wouldn't be happy. But I never thought he'd find it.

I was the one who'd left the layouts out. I had a dentist's appointment and I was late. So I decided I'd come to school early the next day to clean up before Mrs. Hearth got there.

What I didn't know was that Mr. Strickland

had to work late grading papers that day. He kept working until he used up his red pencil, making comments all over people's papers.

He makes comments like, "Awk!" and "Structure?" and "SP!" (which means "spelling is wrong") or "Where did this come from?" or "You can do better!" When you get your paper back from him, it looks like he did more writing than you did. Maybe we should grade him instead!

So he went into Mrs. Hearth's room to borrow a fresh red pencil. And what did he find instead? The almost finished *Real Yearbook*!

Mr. Strickland has no sense of humor. So after seeing our layouts he was really mad! And who was he mad at?

Me, naturally.

The next morning I went in early to clean up. When I didn't see the layouts, I figured Mrs. Hearth had cleaned up for me. So I went to class and sat down.

Everything started out almost normally. The kids all came in, everyone rattled around, talked, put their books away and then sat down. But after Mr. Strickland took attendance, he stood up and smacked his hand down on the pile of stuff on his desk.

I looked at what was under his hand. It was our layouts, and all our other yearbook stuff, too!

My mouth fell open. I looked over at Anthony. His mouth had fallen open, too.

Mr. Strickland looked straight at me.

"Class," he said in his horror-movie voice. "I want every one of you to take a good look at what Amy Erkhardt here has been up to."

He waved a bunch of the pages at us.

"This little batch of work is the most insulting thing I've ever seen!" he said. His voice was getting louder and higher. He should think about singing in a church choir, I thought, instead of teaching sixth grade.

"I found this by accident last evening, and I took it home for a better look," he went on. "Amy Erkhardt has really shown us what she thinks of our wonderful school, and what she thinks of all of you—her classmates."

Everyone in class turned to look at me. Then Mr. Strickland read some of the comments under the pictures out loud.

"Listen to this . . . 'Cyndy Weston: Her hair is fuzzy when it's not curly. But her baton is very twirly!' "

Cyndy started to giggle, but he wasn't listening.

"Or this . . . 'Brad's a jock, his grades are crummy. But his brownies are real yummy!' "

Brad's brownies were the best. Brad looked pleased with himself.

"Or this . . . 'Mr. Strickland shaves his face. Not one hair is out of place. His shirt stays buttoned, his shoes stay tied. He only likes his eggs when fried.' "

That was from the science trip. We thought of it because he was always so neat in the morning, even when he was camping. Also Mr. Strickland had made the cook fry his eggs—special. The rest of us got scrambled eggs. If anyone complained, they got the fish-eye from the counselors *and* Mr. Strickland. Was that fair?

"There's more here, too." By now Mr. Strickland sounded like a fire engine coming down the block. "I want all of you to know what a terrible thing she's done by putting together this yearbook! She's made fun of everyone who made this year a wonderful year for the sixth grade."

Of course, Mr. Strickland didn't know that everyone had worked on *The Real Yearbook.* He also didn't know that each kid wrote his or her own caption.

What Cyndy meant about the frizzy hair

QRSTUVWXYZ

was a joke about how she always sets her hair because she doesn't like it curly. She sets it so it will be straight! But it always gets frizzy again in about half an hour.

Brad was really proud of his brownies. Kids got into fights over who got his brownies instead of mine, for example. My brownies were the worst! And Brad didn't think it was bad that his grades weren't so good. He was proud of being a jock. He was also really proud of being able to make knock-down-drag-out brownies.

"Miss Erkhardt, I want your parents in here tomorrow morning at eight-thirty," said Mr. Strickland. "I already called your mother, young lady, and I'm sure that she's called your father by this time."

Now, this was a problem. My parents had been very quiet around me, and very quiet about the boarding school threats, too. But that didn't mean anything. I knew they were just waiting for something like this. Then they would run right out there and make their threats into a reality.

I may have had all my friends sticking up for me in school, but I wasn't going to have anyone sticking up for me at home tonight.

I also knew that whatever had happened, I

wasn't going to any stupid boarding school. I remembered my promise to myself. I'd run away first.

Reform school, my foot!

That afternoon, when I got home, my mother wasn't there. It didn't matter whether she was home or not. There was no getting away from the fact that my whole life would all blow up at dinner.

But it didn't. My dad came home and we ate, and no one said a word at dinner, either. It was pretty creepy.

I sort of wanted to explain what had happened, but I wasn't going to bring it up if they didn't.

That night I watched TV for a while. When it was time to go to bed, my dad looked at me.

"We'll be taking you to school tomorrow morning," he said. "I'm afraid that you've made one mistake too many. We'll have a talk with your teacher, and then tomorrow night we'll all sit down and decide what to do about you."

I had a few nightmares that night, but nothing I couldn't deal with.

When morning came, I decided to wear my long green skirt from Secondhand Rosalie's, with a black turtleneck. I put on the sweat shirt that I'd cut up and fringed over that. It looked great and I figured, why not? I'd already gotten so far in trouble with my mom and dad, it wouldn't matter what happened at school.

What happened was really amazing.

We met Mr. Strickland in the classroom while the rest of the class was at music class. Mr. Strickland started talking practically before they were in the room.

"Mr. and Mrs. Erkhardt. I want both of you to go over this disgusting, insulting piece of work your daughter is responsible for," he said. "Then we're going to call in the principal. I want everyone to be aware of what's been going on here."

My dad sat down at Mr. Strickland's desk and started reading. He looked really funny sitting there. Mr. Strickland started pacing up and down in front of the desk. The long piece of hair that was supposed to go over the top of his head was hanging over his ear again. My mom frowned at him. I guess she thought he should look neater.

For a few minutes the room was so quiet you could have heard a bug sneeze. Then this funny noise came from my dad. At first I thought he was having trouble breathing.

Great, I thought as I turned to look at him. The Real Yearbook *is giving him a heart attack.*

But Dad wasn't having a heart attack. He had a silly grin on his face. I finally figured out that he was trying not to laugh.

Mr. Strickland didn't understand, either. "You see what I mean?" he said. "Insulting!"

My father turned to the pictures from the science trip.

"Not one hair is out of place, hey?" he said, staring at the top of Mr. Strickland's head.

My mom looked over Dad's shoulder at the picture, and giggled. Mr. Strickland patted the top of his head. I thought he was going to start rubbing his stomach any minute. He quickly flapped his long piece of hair over his bald spot. It didn't work. A long piece of hair still hung over his ear.

Just then, the whole class came trooping back from music. Everyone looked pretty worried when they saw my parents. They knew I was in trouble for something all of us had done. They didn't like the idea that I was the one getting it in the neck.

That's when my dad said it.

"Amy, this is the best thing I've seen in years," he told me. "I wish I'd done something like this when I was a kid. I would have had some really great memories."

Mr. Strickland must not have heard my dad.

Either that or his brain hadn't quite caught up with his mouth yet. That happened to him sometimes.

"See what I mean?" he said. "I knew you'd understand how . . ."

Then he stopped and looked at my mom and dad. They were turning the pages and laughing.

"It's fabulous!" Dad said. "Not only is it a great piece of humor, but it's really a nice, human view of the kids' year."

Everyone in the room started to smile.

"Actually, Dad," I said, now that things didn't look so bad, "I had some help with it. I couldn't have done such a good job by myself."

"Oh, yes?" he said. "Who helped you?"

"Well, Mrs. Hearth thought it would be a nice way for us all to remember our last year of elementary school," I said. "So she gave us advice. And the whole class worked on it, too. Even Mrs. Walters's class."

"Who is Mrs. Hearth?" Mom asked.

"The art teacher," said Mr. Strickland. "And I think I'd like her to come in here, as well as the principal."

"Me, too," said Dad. "I'd like to meet the teacher who can bring out this kind of creativity in children."

Mr. Strickland looked very confused. He'd already said he wanted to get the principal in, so it was too late to back out. But I could see that he was worried. He was getting the idea that maybe his day wasn't going to work out the way he'd thought. With a gloomy look on his face, he sent Brad for both of them.

I guess Mr. Strickland wanted Mrs. Simon to see *The Real Yearbook,* and get everyone—including Mrs. Hearth—in trouble. But, of course, it didn't work out that way.

Mrs. Hearth and Mrs. Simon arrived to find Mom and Dad complimenting all the kids—and me, too! Mrs. Simon examined the yearbook. She was very pleased.

"Be sure to save one for me," she said, patting my head as if I were four years old. Then she turned to Mrs. Hearth. "I think this is a wonderful idea," she said. "Let's do this every year from now on. It's certainly a much better way to make a yearbook!"

Mrs. Hearth smiled. "It was all Amy's idea," she said, "and all the kids helped with the work."

So Mrs. Simon thanked us all again. By the time everyone was finished telling everyone else how great they were, we were all feeling pretty good.

But then the best thing happened.

"This yearbook is so good, kids," Dad said to us all, "I want to buy ad space in it. Not only that, I'm going to tell some of my clients about this thing. That'll definitely pay to have it printed right! And bound! We're going to make *The Real Yearbook* look like a collector's item, kids. How about a gold-stamped cover?"

That was just fine with us. We all cheered and clapped and didn't pay any attention to Mr. Strickland.

Poor Mr. Strickland still couldn't figure out what went wrong!

Chapter 7

The *Real Yearbook* was gorgeous! It looked like a real book! In fact, it was so neat that the kids in the fifth grade wanted one, too.

The librarian put the first copy in a special glass case by the school entrance.

And right on the front page, it said, "Amy Erkhardt, Editor."

My name wasn't the only one there. It also said, "Anthony Williams, Art Editor and Chief of Photography; Mrs. Edith Hearth, Production Supervisor." And it listed all the kids in the sixth grade. We called them contributing editors.

I liked the sound of all those titles.

Other good things happened, too.

When the first copy came out, my parents were really proud of me. They put it on the coffee table in the living room. Every time their friends came over, they dragged out the yearbook and made them read it from cover to cover.

"Take a look at this," my dad would say. "Our little Amy did it. It was all her idea."

It was almost embarrassing after a while. My dad kept one in his office—right in front where the receptionist sits. There was not one more peep about boarding school in our house, either.

My mom did something else really strange and nice. She gave me a present. And it was exactly what I wanted.

"I've enrolled you in a fashion-design class at the art museum," she said. "But you'll have to work hard. It's every Saturday for three hours."

I gave her a big kiss.

"By the way," she added. "I happened to wear one of your T-shirt designs with my tennis shorts at the country club. Now everyone wants one!"

"Great," I said. I could hardly believe it.

"Mrs. Wilson told me she thinks you should have an entire line of designer tennis T-shirts!" she said. "Not bad for someone who isn't even in junior high school yet!"

As you've probably guessed by now, I didn't feel like running away anymore.

But here's the neatest part.

On the last day of school, I decided that I wanted to show all my friends how much I liked them.

I'd been going through my closets with Debbie, looking for stuff to experiment with. In the back of a closet I found a fuzzy pink sweater and a pair of jeans that I hadn't had a chance to cut up or sew lace and brocade all over.

"I'd like to go to school dressed like all my new friends," I said. "Even though it isn't my style. I guess the way everyone else dresses isn't so bad, either. It's just different from mine. People can dress in lots of ways."

"What you wear isn't really who you are," said Debbie. "It's what you think that makes you who you are."

"I know," I said. "I've been thinking about that for a while. Miss Gordon, the teacher in my fashion-design class, said something like that.

"What Miss Gordon said was: 'You aren't always the same person every day. You aren't always doing the same thing every day. There is the perfect outfit for each person . . . and for each activity. That's what makes clothing design so interesting and so fluid.' "

"Sounds like a drink," said Debbie.

"Anyway, she thinks that the fact that people are so different and so interesting and so full of change is what makes fashion design so exciting."

"That's one of the things that makes you so interesting," said Debbie.

After Debbie went home, I thought about that. I realized that before *The Real Yearbook,* I made myself really different on purpose. I wore strange clothes because I thought nobody liked me. If all the other kids were going to push me away and set me apart, I'd make it look as if I wanted to be apart. So I wore clothes that made me strange and different.

I guess it was my way of pushing them away before they had a chance to push me away. That's smart and stupid at the same time.

Now no one was pushing me away anymore. Some days I'm just like Melissa, Cyndy and Ellen. I just didn't want to admit it before.

I only had one more problem. That was

junior high. Next year, three elementary schools would all join together into one junior high school. That meant that even though I'd made a lot of friends this year, next year everything would be different.

All the normal kids from all those normal schools would be in classes with us. I might not end up in any classes with kids I knew.

After thinking about it, I decided maybe I didn't need to wear all those wild, weird clothes all the time. I could always design clothes. I could still fix up my outfits. I just didn't have to make myself so different that I didn't have any friends.

On the last day of school, I wore my fuzzy pink sweater and a pair of jeans.

You would think I'd come in wearing a gorilla costume, the way everyone looked at me.

"Gosh, Amy," said Anthony. "Are you feeling okay?"

I just smiled. "I'm fine, thank you."

But what I was wearing wasn't the big surprise. The big surprise was that everyone else came to school dressed the way I usually did.

Some of the girls had gone to Secondhand Rosalie's. Debbie was wearing a pair of pedal pushers and a halter top. Cyndy wore a long, flowered skirt and a silky black blouse. Emily had on a short black skirt, a black shirt with short sleeves and a pair of black boots!

When we saw each other in class, everyone burst out laughing and started pointing at each other's clothes.

Poor Mr. Strickland turned bright red. But he didn't say anything. I guess he knew when to stay out of trouble.

I looked at Melissa. She'd really "fixed up" her school clothes. She'd cut fringes on the bottom of her skirt and on her blouse.

"Melissa," I said. "Has your mom seen this outfit?"

Melissa smiled. "She helped me do it! By the way, she wants me to ask you how you painted that tennis shirt your mom had. She wants to design some of her own!"

"Next thing you know, everyone at that country club is going to look like a rock star," I said.

There wasn't one person in class dressed the regular way. I had tried to fit into the group, and the group had decided to fit in with me!

And here I was, so afraid to go to junior high school and not have any more friends! I

wasn't going to stick out like a sore thumb anymore. I was part of a group.

"You know what?" I said to Anthony, who peered at me through a pink silk turban. "I bet junior high is going to be a breeze!"